THE Nº1 CAR SPOTTER

Fights the Factory

by Atinuke

illustrated by Warwick Johnson Cadwell

WALKER
BOOKS

First published in Great Britain 2016 by Walker Books Ltd
87 Vauxhall Walk, London SE11 5HJ

2 4 6 8 10 9 7 5 3 1

Text © 2016 by Atinuke
Illustrations © 2016 Warwick Johnson Cadwell

This book has been typeset in Stempel Schneidler and WJCadwell

Printed and bound in Great Britain by Clays Ltd, St Ives plc

British Library Cataloguing in Publication Data:
a catalogue record for this book is
available from the British Library

ISBN 978-1-4063-4347-2

www.walker.co.uk

For Daisy. For Soo. For Erica.
For Justin. For everything. xx
A.

For my gang as ever,
D, S, H and W
I would also like to thank Atinuke and Jacky Paynter
for letting me join No. 1 and his family.
W. JC.

No. 1 Spots a Bugatti

I might look like only a village boy.
A village boy from a no-count village with
no electricity, no school and no shop.

To millions of people, this village might
look like nothing. But here we have the
houses where we sleep, the fields and river
where we grow and catch our food. And we
also have the road.

This village is our home.

And yes, I am a village boy. But not only a village boy. I am the No. 1 car spotter. The No. 1 car spotter in this village.

And the road that passes our village is a No. 1 road! It speeds past on its way from one metropolis to another. It carries many lorries and buses and taxis. And it carries many fine-fine cars too.

WAIT! What can I hear?

An engine! A car! A car is coming! And by the sound of this engine, it is not just a battered up Peugeot taxi that is approaching. No! I can hear...

Not a Mercedes Benz. Not a BMW. What is it? An engine I have never heard before!

I lean out from the palm tree – then I see it. A car I have never seen before on this road. A car I saw only once in a picture torn from a city magazine. I shout its name for the entire village to hear.

"BUGATTI! BUGATTI! BUGATTI!"

My best friend,
Coca-Cola, comes
running out of his
mother's chop-house.
My cousins Emergency and
Tuesday come running up from the river.
Even my sister, Sissy, puts her head over our
compound wall to look.

I climb down from the tree and run to the
road. We are all running alongside the car,
screaming and shouting and waving.

"BUGATTI! BUGATTI! BUGATTI!"

Never has such a fine-fine car rolled past
our village!

And I should know! I have seen uncountable
Peugeots, I have seen many Mercedes Benz,
I have even seen some Lamborghinis. But I have
never before in my life seen a Bugatti Veron!

NA-WA-OH! WOW!

Coca-Cola and Emergency and Tuesday and I are jumping up and down, up and down.

"Super fine! Super fine!" Coca-Cola punches the air.

"So shiny! So sleeeeeeek!" Emergency is almost singing.

"Dust did not dare even to touch that car!" Tuesday marvels.

"LAZY BOY!" Coca-Cola's mother shouts from the chop-house for him to come and carry drinks for her customers.

"WHERE ARE YOU?" Uncle Go-Easy shouts for my cousins to come and drag the nets from the river.

"OYA, COME NOW!"

Grandfather shouts for me from under the
iroko tree.

We scatter! But we are still shouting about
that car!

"It must have been a chief's car!" Coca-
Cola shouts as he runs.

"A chief?" Emergency is shouting over
his shoulder. "That car could only have
belonged to a singer..."

"And his girlfriend!" Tuesday gives his
brother a high-five.

I roll my eyes. Who cares what person
is inside a car? It is the car that
matters!

"Bugatti! Bugatti!" I
pant when I arrive at
Grandfather's tree.
"Did you see it,
Grandfather?"
"I saw it! I saw it!"

11

Grandfather's grin is so wide it splits his face in two. "I never knew I would be so lucky as to see one of those!"

It was Grandfather who taught me everything I know about car spotting. When he was a boy, there was no road here. And when he was a young man, the only car on the road was the Peugeot 404. Now Grandfather has been lucky enough to see a Bugatti Veron.

And, unbelievably, in less than two hours' time we are all lucky again – the Bugatti Veron returns! Where was it going so close to here that it returned so quick?

This time as I run alongside the car I look inside. There is a man shouting into a mobile phone. An open briefcase is next to him on the seat.

"That is not a chief!" I tell the others. "That is not a music star! That is a businessman!"

"Grandmother! Grandfather!" It is Mama shouting now.

She is turning away from a taxi. The taxi that brings us news of my father in the city. Then she is running up to the village, still shouting! I run after her. Grandmother comes hurrying from the compound. Grandfather stands up under the tree.

"News from Femi!" Mama is laughing and crying all at once. "He has sold his business in the city. He is coming home!"

Grandmother's and Grandfather's eyes light up. Grandmother and Grandfather grasp each other's hands.

Femi is their son, and he is my father.
He lives in the city, earning money by
wheelbarrowing peoples' possessions from
the bus stations to their homes. He sends
the money home to us.
But now he is coming
back himself!

"Coming home!"
Grandmother
exclaims.

Then she
frowns and throws her
arms open wide. "For what?"

We look around at our dry and dusty
village. At the crooked houses, bleating
goats and raggedy children. What job is
there here for a man with a wife, two
children and two parents to support?

Uncle Go-Easy sells fish from the river
by the side of the road – and he only just
makes enough money to survive.

"Femi sent a message to say there is a factory opening near here! He says there will be work. Plenty of work for everybody!" Mama is so excited she is shouting.

Mama grasps my hands and dances in a circle. Grandfather laughs. And Grandmother falls on her knees in praise.

Since the news came we have never been so happy!

Everything my sister Sissy and I say begins with "When Papa comes home…"

Sometimes we both say it at the same time. Then we both laugh. Can you imagine? Sissy and I laughing together! That is the kind of miracle my father can produce!

I find myself smiling when I am groaning under a load of firewood for the cooking fires. I know my father will help lift the load onto my head. Even when I am struggling to herd the long-horned cows back from the river.

I smile. I know my father will be proud
of me controlling these cows alone. Even
when I am creeping
through the dark
night to the toilet,
thinking of snakes.
Even then I smile.
I know when he
returns, my father
will chase all the
snakes away with a big stick.

The day before my father's return, Mama
cooks so much food that Grandmother
laughs.

"Femi loves to eat!" my mother protests.
"I want there to be enough."

Grandmother laughs again.

"I know my son loves to eat but even
he cannot eat ten yams and a goat all by
himself!"

My mother looks around at the many

pans of yam and stews and goat meat ready
for frying. Then she laughs too.

"So let us invite everybody!" she says.
"Let us invite the whole village!"

And Grandmother is so happy that she
does!

On arrival day Sissy and I are waiting
down by the road before dawn. And
we are not the only ones. I can see
Grandfather sitting under the iroko tree
with Grandmother beside him. And Mama
is already lighting her cooking fires. We all
know that my father will not have even left
the city by now. But we want to be ready to
greet him.

As soon as I hear a taxi engine coming
from the direction of the city, I run down
the road with Sissy on my heels. Many-
many taxis pass but my father is not in
any of them.

Dawn comes, the sun climbs high in the sky.

Grandmother
does not call us to
collect firewood
or take the goats
to the bush.
Mama does
not call us

to eat. Sissy and I continue to run towards
each and every taxi, with sweat running
down our backs. Everybody is waiting to
hear us shout "Papa!"

The sun is past its highest point. My best
friend, Coca-Cola, comes to the road.

"How goes?" he asks us.

"We are still waiting," I answer.

Mama Coca-Cola come out of her
roadside chop-house restaurant. She gives
us some akara she says is burnt.

I can see my Uncle Go-Easy and my
cousins Emergency and Tuesday and Nike
watching us from the river. From time to

time Nike brings us water to drink.

And every time we hear an engine the heads of everybody in the village pop up over their compound walls.

The sun starts its descent towards nightfall. The smells coming from our compound make my stomach growl. Sissy's stomach growls too. We smile at each other.

Then I hear another taxi. We jog slowly towards the oncoming car. I see an arm resting on the taxi door through the open window. An arm that waves as the road bends towards the village.

"PAPA!" I roar.

"PAPAAAA!" Sissy screams.

We run along beside the taxi, looking into my father's gleaming, beaming face. The taxi stops outside the chop-house. Mama is already there. Papa grabs all of us at once, Mama and Sissy and me.

We are laughing and crying all together.

That night is the most wonderful night of my life. We laugh and eat, eat and laugh. Mama and Grandmother sing so loud that the whole village dances

until morning! And best of all, Papa is there. I hear his laugh mingle with ours. I see his praise makes Mama's eyes shine. I feel his arm around my back when I sit beside him. Life cannot get more wonderful than this!

The following day my father takes us to see the factory. It is on the other side of the town. For weeks now all the talk at market has been about factory, factory, factory. And for weeks now I have been trying to slip away to see what this factory is. But every time I try, Grandmother catches me by my ear.

"Do you think that I do not know where you are going?" she shouts. "Factories are not for small boys like you. Your job is to help your grandmother."

But this time Papa waves Grandmother off.

"I want my son to see where his father will be working!"

I am so proud I grow taller right then and there! And when I see the factory –

NA-WA-OH!!!!!

It is higher than ten schools all piled one on top of each other. It is wider than my whole entire village with all our compounds! It has pipes reaching high into the sky. And pipes going straight into the river. A tall wire fence surrounds it. A fence patrolled by men with crazy-looking dogs. I have never seen such a building!

On the day that the factory opens, the whole village is there outside that fence. My father is waiting at the gates with the other people from villages who have been given employment.

I am jumping up and down. Trying to see
my father. I want to see him enter the gates.
Then I hear an engine! An engine I know
now!
"BUGATTI!" I shout.
The big fat shiny Bugatti Veron speeds
along the road. The factory gates magically
open and the car passes into the
factory compound!

I cannot believe it!
I had forgotten all about the Bugatti. And
what it was doing so near to our village.

I had forgotten because I was too busy thinking about my father's return.

That car and Papa's return had seemed two completely unrelated events. But it was not so! That car is connected to the factory. The factory that has brought my father home!

I have spotted the car. I have spotted the factory. And when I spot the man climbing out from the Bugatti and addressing the workers, I guess that he is the man who owns this factory. The man who brought my father home. The man who has made my whole family happier than we have ever been before.

"That man," I say to Sissy, "is my hero!"

What Will We Eat Now?

I am the No. 1 car spotter. And
  Grandfather says the reason that I
  am the No. 1 car spotter is because
  I have a No. 1 brain.

    But it was not until I saw the
Bugatti drive inside the factory
compound with my own two eyes
that I put the two and two together.

    "My brain is getting very slow,"
I confide in Grandfather. "I am no
longer sure that it is, in fact, No. 1."

    Grandfather laughs.

"Maybe it has only got lazy," he says.
"It needs a good problem to wake it up."

I open my mouth to answer Grandfather.
But then I hear...
"FIREBIRD!"
The Firebird is the one and only Pontiac
Firebird in our whole country!

I run towards the road shouting:
"FIREBIRD! FIREBIRD! FIREBIRD!"
The Firebird slows and stops. A small man
holding a newspaper gets out of the car.

"Greetings, Prof." I prostrate myself.
"How is your wife? And your
children?"

"Get up, No. 1." Prof smiles.
"They are well."

Then Prof looks at my
big-big smile.

"Waytin' happen?"
he asks.

"My father has returned." I smile and smile. "He has returned from the city. He is working in a factory. A factory close to here!"

"This is excellent news, No. 1!" Prof smiles too. "I have heard about this factory. It is one of the Temi-Tola factories. You people are very lucky that Chief Temi-Tola decided to build one of his factories right here."

"Chief Temi-Tola?" I say. "Does he drive a Bugatti?"

Prof looks at me.

"No. 1," he says. "This obsession with cars—"

"A red Bugatti Veron?" I interrupt.

"I do not know..." Prof throws his arms wide.

Then he smiles. "Look."

Prof opens the newspaper under his arm. There is a photograph of a man climbing out of a Bugatti.

"That is it!" I shout. "That is him! My hero!"

The Bugatti Veron belongs to Chief Temi-Tola! So Coca-Cola and I were both right. The Bugatti belongs to a man who is both a chief and a businessman.

Prof shakes the newspaper and starts to read:

"'Chief Temi-Tola is one of the richest and most powerful men in our country. Maybe one of the richest and most powerful men in the whole of Africa. He owns not only factories, but oil refineries as well. He has been opening new factories all over the country.'"

"And he has been here!" I say to Prof. "In his Bugatti. I have seen it with my own two eyes!"

Prof laughs.

"Are you more excited

to see the man or the car?" he asks.

I look at Prof. I am confused. It is the car that is wonderful to see, of course!

"And do you know what this factory produces?" Prof asks me.

I shrug my shoulders. It does not make anything useful, like shoes or pencils or sugar. My father has told us that. Even he does not know what it is that this factory produces.

"It is a pesticide." Prof shakes his newspaper. "That is what it says here. It is transforming the farming industry."

I look at Prof. "What is this pes-pes—?"

"A pesticide is something farmers spray on their fields," he explains. "It kills all the weeds and all the insects. When a farmer

 sprays with pesticide, nothing grows in the field apart from the crop."

My eyes open wide. Can this be true?

My mother works in our fields every single day. Every single day she removes the weeds that threaten to smother our crops. She removes them one by one by one. And while she is doing that she has to kill the insects that want to eat our crops too. She kills them one by one by one. It is a never-ending battle that Mama is always on the point of losing.

But now this factory is making something that will kill weeds and insects all at once! *Na-wa-oh!*

I drag Prof to the iroko tree to explain the whole thing to Grandfather. Grandfather is so excited that he pounds his stick on the ground. The shells on his stick rattle and everybody in the village gathers to hear what Grandfather has to say.

"Next year we will be rich!" Grandfather announces. "Next year we will be fat! Fat husbands, fat wives, fat children."

Everybody starts smiling and clapping.

"But how can this be?" Grandmother asks.

Grandfather gestures to Prof.

"Explain it to them!" he says.

"The factory is producing a pesticide," Prof pontificates. "This product will rid your fields of all pests and enable your crops to grow without hindrance."

Everybody is looking at Prof as if he was speaking a foreign language.

Who here can understand words such as "pesticide" or "hindrance"? It is not as if English is the one and only language that we are speaking. It is not even our first language!

I look at everybody's blank and confused faces. I interrupt Prof. I speak the English we speak in our village so that they can understand.

"Dis factory-o!" I say. "Dis factory no

be one ordinary factory. Dis factory make sometin' that go make our village fat! Sometin' dey call pesta-killa."

Everybody's eyes start to shine.

"How?" Emergency shouts.

"How? How?" Everybody is shouting.

I shout back:

"Because dis pest-a-killa get power to kill every weed for field dat try to overtake our crop!"

Everybody gasps.

"Not only this!"

My voice grows even louder. "Dis powaful pest-a-killa can kill any type of catapilla or whatever dat try to chop our crop!"

Auntie Fine-Fine starts to ululate. Mama B starts to cry. She gathers her children, Beke, Bisi and Bola, into her arms. Her tears fall on their thin arms and skinny legs.

"Next year you will be fat!" Mama B cries. "Next year you will eat and eat and eat!"

"Did I not tell you?" Grandfather says. "You had to wait for a small boy to explain it to you!"

Everybody laughs. And Prof shakes his head.

"No. 1," he says, "you should come and give my lectures at the university. Then nobody would yawn and complain about incomprehensibility. I would become the most popular teacher on the campus."

That night the whole village dances and sings again. And every single woman cooks a mountain of food without worrying about running out.

"Because by next year we will all be buying this pest-a-killa. We will grow so much food we will never worry about running out again," Mum says.

Sissy and I do not sleep long before Mama wakes us for school the next morning. We do not care that we are tired. Our happiness powers our feet all the way to school. Only Coca-Cola groans.

"My feet were already paining me before I even stood on them this morning," he complains. "I danced too much last night!"

Sissy and I laugh.

"Why are you two laughing all the time?" Coca-Cola frowns.

Sissy and I look at each other.

"Papa is home," I say.

"And Mama is singing all the time," Sissy says.

"And Grandmother has stopped shouting at us," I say.

"Yes!" Sissy agrees. "She is too busy now, smiling at Papa."

"And next year we will all grow fat!" I put my arm through Coca-Cola's. "You will be so fat the ground will shake when you dance and your feet will pain you every day!"

And this time Coca-Cola laughs too.

We laugh so much that day that our teacher complains. And all the way home we joke about all the food we will eat next year.

"I will eat a mountain of yam with my fish stew every night!" I say.

"I will eat a mountain of plantain with fried fish before I even start for school!" Coca-Cola says.

We shake our heads. Imagine! Eating in the morning!

Then Sissy says, "I will carry food to school to eat. Rice with smoked fish."

We all laugh at the thought of eating food at school! Imagine eating, eating, eating all day long!

But when we return to the village our smiling and laughing is quenched.

The whole village is silent. There is no smoke from cooking fires. No laughing or singing coming from behind the compound walls. It is empty under the iroko tree.

"Mama?" Coca-Cola calls as we near the chop-house.

There is silence. Sissy and Coca-Cola and I look at one another.

Where is Mama Coca-Cola? Where is everybody? What has happened?

Sissy starts to run up to the village.

"Mama? Mama?" she is shouting.

I hear a sound. I turn towards the river.

"Sissy!" I shout. And start to run.

The whole village is gathered by the water's edge. Nobody turns to greet us. Not even Mama. I push in.

Floating on the river-water are fish.
Big fish. Small fish. Silver fish. Grey fish.
All dead fish. This is bad.

My body is frozen. My eyes are staring.
My brain malfunctions. It can think only
one thought.

The fish are dead! The fish are dead!

And my brain cannot understand how
this one thought could possibly be true. The
only sound is Uncle Go-Easy weeping. Until
suddenly Mama moans.

"What will we eat?"

And suddenly everybody wails. I am stiff
with fear. We are not rich people. We cannot
eat chicken or goat every day. If we did, our
animals would soon be gone. And we do
not have money to buy meat. Some days we
eat the beans that we grow in our fields. But
most days we eat fish.

Fish are free. When they are alive and
healthy, all we have to do is fish for them
and they are good to eat.

Uncle Go-Easy falls down on the river-
bank. How will he support his family now?

"What is happening here, people?"

It is the voice of the American engineer, Mr Johnson. I had heard his car. But the part of my brain that spots cars no longer seems to be connected to my body. All I can do is stare at the dead fish.

And it seems that everybody's brain has disconnected. Nobody turns. Nobody answers Mr Johnson. All we can do is watch the dead fish floating by.

Mr Johnson shoulders his way to the river's edge. Then he is silent too.

"How could dis happen?" Uncle Go-Easy's voice is high and thin.

"Those fish have been poisoned."
Mr Johnson sounds angry.

"But why?" Mama's
voice is thick with
tears. "Why would
somebody poison our fish?"

"Who?" Emergency sounds so angry.
"Who did this?"

Mr Johnson is silent. He has no answers.

That night, when my father returns from
work, we run to him. But he has no answers
either. All we have are questions.

"Who did this? Why?"

And most important of all, "What will we
eat now?"

Wake Up Your Brain

I am the No. 1 car spotter. I know everything there is to know about Honda and Audi and Lamborghini. I can speak my mother's language and my father's language and I speak English as well. I can recite many stories from our oral tradition. And I know *A* to *Z* and also 1 to infinity.

But I do not know why the fish in the river are dying.

Every morning Grandmother looks at me.

"No. 1," she says. "We need you now. Wake up your brain."

Grandmother's face is as hard as iron. But there are rivers of tears behind her voice.

Grandmother has never asked me to do anything before other than to collect wood or water the goats. Never before has she believed in the power of my brain.

I think and think but achieve no electricity for brain. Now every morning I avoid Grandmother's eyes. This is the first time she has believed in me and I am failing her.

"Leave the boy." Mama weeps. "This problem is too big for him. It is too big for all of us."

I look at the ground. There was once a time when I believed that no problem was too big for me. When I took on leopards and cars thieves and floods without hesitation.

But now I am too hungry to think. I do not know what to do.

"Just tell me who did it," says Emergency to me, "and I will deal with him."

But I do not know. Maybe my brain needs
fish to power it.

We walk to school hungry. We sit at our
tables with our stomachs complaining.
And we know that when we lie down
to sleep we will still be hungry after
eating only a small portion of yam
and vegetable.

After school I walk up to the
iroko tree. Grandfather
is there. He looks at
my face.

"Waytin', No. 1?"
he asks.

"Everybody wants me to find a solution."
I try not to cry.

Grandfather looks at me with his old
watery eyes.

"And?" he asks.

"And I cannot!" I cry out. "I cannot find
the answer! I have not one single idea!"

Grandfather closes his eyes.

"What do you know
about, No. 1?" he asks.

I think about
Grandfather's question
before I answer.

"I know about
spotting cars," I say slowly.
"And about herding goats. And
catching fish. And climbing
palm trees. I know nouns and
verbs and multiplication and
addition. And I know many
stories from the Odu Ifa."

I finish. There is silence.

"You know about the road and the village and the bush," Grandfather says at last.

"And school," I say. "I know about school."

Grandfather nods.

"Is it somebody in the village who is poisoning the fish?" he asks.

I shake my head. Of course not. Who in the village would want to starve?

"Is it somebody at school?"

I shake my head again. Everybody at school lives along the river. We are all starving together.

"To solve the problem of the car thieves you had to go to the city," Grandfather says. "Because that is where the car thieves were. The car thieves did not come from the village."

I look at Grandfather. He looks back at me with his old-old eyes.

"The solution to this problem is not here either," Grandfather says.

"But where, Grandfather?" I ask. "Where is the solution?"

Grandfather closes his eyes.

"You are the No. 1 problem solver," he says. "Not me."

I look at Grandfather. His eyes remain shut. I know he will say no more. I sigh loudly.

After a while I walk down to the road. If the problem is not in the village, it must be somewhere along the road.

As I walk I see someone coming towards me. It is my father! Returning from work. I run to take his lunch bucket. We walk back to the village together. From time to time my father coughs.

Mr Johnson's Hummer passes us on the

road. When we arrive back in the village, it is parked outside the chop-house. We are about to enter when we hear Grandmother scream.

Papa runs towards our compound. I follow him. I can hear Grandmother shouting and crying. People are running from all directions towards our compound. Even Mr Johnson is running behind me.

In the compound Grandmother is wailing. She is standing over the goats. And every single goat has its head hanging and its belly heaving and its mouth frothing.

Goats are our only wealth. Prof has explained to me all about banks where rich people store their money to use when they need it. Our goats are like that for us. As long as we look after them, they multiply all by themselves. And in an emergency, if we need money for medicine or a wedding or for school shoes, we can sell some goats in order to pay.

Mr Johnson is on his knees, looking into the mouths of the goats.

"These goats have been poisoned!" he says.

"You said that about the fish!"
Grandmother shouts.

Mama turns on Mr Johnson. "Is that all you can say?"

Papa leans against the compound wall coughing.

"Leave him," he says sadly. "He is right."
Grandmother wails as loudly as if she has stepped on a burning branch. She turns on Sissy.

"You were herding the goats this afternoon," she says. "Where did you go? What did they eat?"

"I only went into the bush," she says. "As far as the big rocks. Where we always go. Then to the river. So that they could drink."

I turn to look towards the river. And it is in that moment that I finally achieve electricity for brain!

The river! The river where the fish swam! The river where the goats drank!

"It is the river!" I shout. "The river is poisoned!"

There is silence. Then suddenly everybody is shouting all at once – Grandmother, Grandfather, Mama, Auntie Fine-Fine, Uncle Go-Easy, Mama B, Mama Coca-Cola.

The river where we drink. Where we collect water for cooking. Where we wash our clothes. Where we swim.

"But why?" Emergency punches the compound wall.

"Who would do such a thing?" Auntie Fine-Fine is sobbing.

My brain is on fire. Papa is still coughing.

The answer is not in the village. Grandfather told me that. It's somewhere else. Somewhere along the road. The road where I walked to meet my father. My father returning from the factory.

Suddenly a light bulb goes off inside my head. And I see again what I had seen when my father had taken me there – the pipes from the factory going straight into the river!

"The factory is poisoning the river!" The words rush from my mouth.

Immediately there is silence. A different silence. Papa stares at me.

"No. 1, what did you say?" Grandfather asks slowly.

"Repeat yourself!" shouts Grandmother.

"Crazy boy!" shouts Auntie Fine-Fine.

Now everybody in the village is shouting that I am an idiot. An ignorant and stupid boy. Everybody except Papa. Papa is still staring at me.

Mr Johnson puts his hand on my shoulder.

"Why do you say that, boy? Why do you say that the factory is poisoning the river?"

And even though everybody thinks that I am a stupid ignorant idiot ye-ye boy, everybody listens to my answer.

"Because there are pipes from the factory that go into the river. Big pipes. And because the fish started dying after the factory opened."

Everybody turns to look at my father.

"Femi, can this be true?" Grandmother whispers.

Suddenly Papa looks small. He is silent, with his hands over his eyes.

"Femi!" Mama shouts so loudly that I jump. "Speak to us! Tell us the truth!"

"In the factory we make a powder which goes into containers. But out of the machine that makes the powder there is a watery something. That something goes into pipes that empty into the river."

Only after he has spoken does Papa take his hands down from his eyes.

"I did not realize until the boy said it," he says slowly. "But it must be true. It is the factory that is poisoning the river."

There is a long silence. Then Mr Johnson speaks loudly.

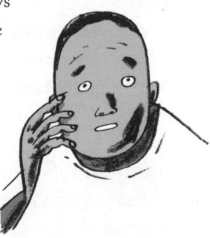

"But there are rules! There are rules about the disposal of chemicals."

"Not in this here Africa," Papa says.

"Yes. Here in Africa. There are rules," Mr Johnson insists.

Papa shrugs his shoulders.

"I will go to see the factory owner," Mr Johnson says.

"Chief Temi-Tola?" I ask incredulously.

"Yes." Mr Johnson nods vigorously.

The whole village looks at one another.

"What will you do to him?" Emergency asks.

Mr Johnson laughs. "I will talk to him!"

"Oh!" Emergency is disappointed.

"You must be careful," Grandfather says. "You must be careful not to anger the man."

"Anger him?" Mr Johnson says. "He has angered me!"

"And me!" says Mama.

"And me!" says Mama Coca-Cola.

And even Uncle Go-Easy says, "And me!"

"You must still be careful," Grandfather insists.

But nobody is listening to Grandfather. The men carry Mr Johnson down to his car, shouting encouragement. I sit and cry. Chief Temi-Tola was my hero. But I was wrong. Chief Temi-Tola is no hero.

It is weeks before Mr Johnson returns.
During those weeks there is no time to go
to school. No time to go to the fields. No
time to stand at the road spotting cars.

There is only time for trekking to
water, queuing for water, carrying
water.

We do not dare drink at the
river now. Or collect water to
cook there or even wash our
clothes there.

So we have to trek into the
bush to the only water pipe.
We have to wait in turn with all the other
villages to pump water for our goats and
cows to drink, to pump
water to wash our
clothes, to pump
water to fill our
water containers
to carry home all

the water we need for
cooking and drinking.

And in the hot, dry,
dusty bush there are
no cars to spot and no
lessons to learn.

"How will I become
a teacher if I cannot go to school?" Sissy
weeps.

"How will you become a teacher if you
drink poisoned river-water?" Grandmother
snaps.

Worst of all, we cannot carry enough
water for our fields. And we do not dare
water our crops with the river-water.
So we are watching our crops die.
And if the pest-a-killa
comes next year it will
be of no use to us
who have no water
to irrigate our fields.

So we queue for water with our heads bowed. Only the thought of Mr Johnson keeps any hope alive.

"He will make that factory owner behave himself," Grandmother says. "He will restore health to the river. And bring our goats back to life."

"You think Mr Johnson can bring goats back to life?" Grandfather raises his eyebrows. "He is only an American! He can't work miracles!"

Grandmother opens her mouth to argue.

"He is a Westerner," Grandfather continues. "He does not understand Africa. He is going to cause trouble for us all."

Grandfather walks away. I look from him to Grandmother. I have never seen them argue before. It pains my heart.

Luckily at that moment I hear something. "HUMMER! HUMMER! HUMMER!"

The whole village rushes to the road. Even Grandfather. We usher Mr Johnson into the chop-house. Mama Coca-Cola starts to fry akara for free.

But Mr Johnson does not look happy.

"Did you see him?" Mama asks.

"Did you tell him about my goats?" asks Grandmother.

"Did you tell him about the fish?" asks Uncle Go-Easy.

Mr Johnson puts his mobile phone down on the table.

"I made an appointment to see Chief Temi-Tola at his head office," Mr Johnson tells us. "I told him everything that is happening here. Everything! And I told him that there are rules and regulations about the disposal of factory waste. Here in Africa, I told him, the rules and regulations are strict!"

"Yes? Yes?" asks Grandmother.

"He laughed at me!" Mr Johnson explodes. "He laughed in my face. He told me that I did not understand how things are done here in Africa."

Grandfather closes his eyes.

"He told me the officials who enforce the rules about chemical waste disposal are not paid properly. He told me those men cannot even afford to buy cars to go to inspect factories. Chief Temi-Tola told me he is generous with those men. He buys them cars. On the condition that they do not drive them in the direction of his factories.

"They approve his factories without even visiting them." Mr Johnson's voice cracks. "He told me that to my face! With pride!"

Suddenly Mr Johnson's eyes are bright with tears of rage. "And now my visa has been revoked!" he cries. "Soon I will have to leave the country. Why is Africa so corrupt?"

Nobody says anything. Grandfather's eyes remain closed.

My father walks into the silent chop-
house. He is carrying his lunch bucket.
Mr Johnson stares at the bucket.

"What is that?" He points.

"It is an empty bucket from the factory,"
Papa says.

Mr Johnson is staring
at the bucket as if it
will run across the
floor and bite him.

"But that substance
is banned in the US!"
he says. "It poisons
every living thing."

He looks more
closely at the bucket.

"'Made in the US,'" he reads. "For export
only."

"The whole world is corrupt," Grandfather
says bitterly.

After that nobody wants to say anything.

Mr Johnson gets into his car and drives away. People go back to their compounds.

I help Coca-Cola to clean the chop-house for his mother. I find Mr Johnson's mobile phone!

"Mr Johnson!" I shout. "Wait!"

I run out of the door and up the road. But Mr Johnson has gone. Even the dust on the road has settled.

I shrug my shoulders. I put his phone in my pocket. I will return it to him next time he comes.

Bulldozers

I am the No. 1 car spotter. And I have a
No. 1 problem. I lie awake thinking about
this problem and listening to Papa coughing.

The man who I thought was my hero is
in fact my enemy. And how can I stop him
from poisoning our river, our fish, our goats,
our crops?

This problem is bigger than me. It has
me thrashing about on my mat like a snake
under a stick until Sissy kicks me.

"How can anybody sleep with you
agitating all night?" she hisses.

So I give up worrying and start thinking about something else. Like why Papa is coughing-coughing-coughing all the time.

No! That is something else that I do not want to think about.

I must think of something else. Like how in my trouser pocket I have an American phone. That phone can do anything. It is a camera, a video machine, a television, a games console, a computer – and one can also use it for making calls or sending texts.

I know because Mr Johnson's son, LeRoy, has a phone like that and he has shown me

everything that it can do.

And now I – I, the No. 1 car spotter – I have one in my trouser pocket! And my fingers are itching to turn it on.

It is exactly at this moment that I hear a sound which makes me jump up from my mat.

I look out of the window. It is dawn. The sound is coming from the road. But it is not a car! What is it?

I pull on my trouser and run outside. The noise is getting louder and louder and louder!

Then from around the corner comes another machine that I have only ever seen in a magazine.

"BULLDOZER!" I shout, jumping up and down. "BULLDOZER! BULLDOZER!"

And not just one bulldozer. One, two, three bulldozers! I jump up and down waiting to watch the bulldozers pass.

But they do not pass.

They turn off the road and start crawling up to the village.

I stand stupid with my mouth hanging open until the first bulldozer barrels into Auntie Fine-Fine's compound wall.

"*Yee! Yee! Ewu mbo! Jamba mbo!*" I scream in my mother tongue. They are the first words that come to my lips.

Help! Warning! Danger!

Then I am racing back to the village.
Screaming and shouting.
And I am running into our
compound. And I am pulling
Sissy from her mat. And I
can hear my Auntie Fine-
Fine scream. And suddenly
everybody is screaming and
shouting and running and crying.

I run out of our house with Grandfather
on my back. When
Grandfather sees the
bulldozers he wails
and lets go of my
neck. Grandfather
falls on the ground.

The bulldozers have flattened
Auntie Fine-Fine's
compound wall!
Her goats are
scattering.

Papa is climbing up one of the bulldozers. The driver is in a glass cage. My father is pounding on the glass. He cannot break it open.

Uncle Go-Easy is running from house to house. Chasing out the children. Grandmother is pulling Grandfather along the ground. She is screaming too.

Then over the sound of bulldozers and crying and screaming I hear another sound.

BUGATTI!

The Bugatti is stopping. Chief Temi-Tola is coming out. The man who was once my hero is smiling! He is clapping!

"Troublemakers!" he shouts. "You see what I do to troublemakers!"

My body acts on its own accord. I take Mr Johnson's phone from my pocket.

I switch on the video camera.

I press RECORD.

I record the bulldozers. Destroying our compound walls. I record our goats. Disappearing into the bush.

I record Beke and Bisi and Bola. Screaming and running in fear.

I record Uncle Go-Easy. Falling with Coca-Cola's grandmother on his back.

78

I record Chief Temi-Tola. Laughing.

I record it all.

After a while the Chief waves the bulldozers away.

"This is a lesson for you troublemakers!" he shouts. "Next time it will be your houses that I destroy."

Then he laughs and climbs back into his car. The Buggati drives away. Slowly the bulldozers follow.

I press STOP.

Then I go to YouTube. I know LeRoy's password.

I hesitate.

I hear LeRoy's voice in my head: "Just do it, bro."

So I do what my American friend, Mr Johnson's son, LeRoy, used to do when he wanted his American friends to see what he was doing here in our African village.

I enter the password.

I think of words I have learned at school.

I write CHIEF TEACHES VILLAGE A LESSON.

I press UPLOAD.

Now at least LeRoy and his friends will know what has happened to us.

That night nobody sleeps. Once we had food in our village, we had shelter, we were safe. Now we have no food, no water. Now we are not safe. People sit in our house, waiting for Grandfather to tell them what to do. But Grandfather is crying.

I lie down beside Papa. I always feel safe and strong when I am near Papa. But I do not feel safe and strong now. Papa is coughing and coughing. And I feel afraid.

I could not stop the the factory poisoning the river. I could not stop it poisoning the goats. Or poisoning the fish.

And I could not stop it poisoning my father either. I know why Papa is coughing.

"It is like the factory gas is trapped inside here," he says, clutching his chest.

Mama weeps.

Over the following days people start to leave for the city. Grandmother refuses to let us go. If those people cannot find work they will become beggars. But can we stay here with no goats, no crops, no fish, no water?

I hear the Firebird stop outside the chophouse. I do not shout. I do not even get up. Prof enters. He is smiling and grinning and waving a newspaper. What is wrong with him? Can he not see what has happened to us?

Prof clasps Grandfather's trembling hands.

"Baba." He smiles. "All is not lost! The President is on his way!"

Grandfather looks at Prof with blank eyes. We all do. What has

the President got to do with us?

Prof shakes out his newspaper and starts to read.

"'Yesterday Chief Temi-Tola was arrested for his crimes against a small rural village.'"

I stare at Prof. We all stare at Prof.

"'Thirty million people worldwide called for the arrest of the Chief after witnessing him laughing as he wrecked the village.'"

Prof looks up.

"The whole world is on your side!" he

says. "People have been tweeting from China, from the UK, from South Africa, from Australia, from Kenya, from America, from all over Nigeria.

"Thirty million of them, all sending messages on their mobile phones. They forced our President to act! Chief Temi-Tola is in jail and he is not coming out!"

Thirty million people?

Are there even thirty million people in this world?

Grandmother shakes her head.

"What are you saying?" she asks, confused.

Mr Johnson's SUV comes speeding down the road. He jumps out and straight into the chop-house. He throws me up into the air.

"What a hero!" Mr Johnson shouts.

Now I am confused. What did I do?

Suddenly Grandmother grabs Mr Johnson's shoulder in one hand. She grabs Prof's arm in the other. She shakes them both like small children.

"What are you talking about?" she shouts.

"Somebody took a video," Prof says quickly. "A video of the village being destroyed. A video of Chief Temi-Tola laughing.

Then that somebody sent out that video on the internet, where anybody in the world could look at it. And more than thirty million people looked."

All of a sudden my eyes open wide. I only put that video there for Leroy and his friends. Not for thirty million people!

Grandmother narrows her eyes.

"Who was this somebody?" she asks.

Mr Johnson looks at me. Slowly I take his phone from my pocket.

"Mr Johnson," I say nervously. "You left your phone in the chop-house. I was looking after it for you, but then..."

"But then you took a video of Chief Temi-Tola and his bulldozers!" shouts Mr Johnson. "Brilliant! Brilliant!"

Both Mr Johnson and Prof are grinning all over their faces.

Now Grandmother turns on me. She is so confused, her mouth opens, then closes. I try to explain.

"I just wanted Leroy to know," I say.

"All Leroy's friends showed their parents. And all their parents showed their friends. Until more than thirty million people saw!" says Mr Johnson.

Grandmother opens her mouth again but Prof speaks first.

"You are a hero, No. 1," he says. "My hero!"

It is then we hear the sirens. The presidential convoy is arriving! And with it vans marked CNN and NEWSFLASH.

"The President is coming to right your wrongs." Prof looks at Grandfather. "You must prepare yourselves."

Grandfather looks dazed and confused. But Grandmother nods her head. She turns to us all.

"We have suffered," she says. "That does not mean that we cannot stand tall."

Grandmother walks down to the road and the whole village follows her.

"I greet you, my President," Grandmother says. "I welcome you to my village. It has no fish, no crops, no goats, no compounds. But still we welcome you."

In our torn and dusty clothes we sing the song we use to welcome important visitors. When we have finished, the President is silent. Then he wipes his eyes.

"You are a brave people," he says. "And your suffering has not gone unnoticed. I am here to help you. Tell me what you need."

The news cameras roll. And Grandmother stands tall.

"Our compounds are broken."

Grandmother waves her arms. "And our goats have scattered."

"Our river is poisoned." Uncle Go-Easy points.

"Our fish are dead."

"And we have no water pump!" shouts Mama Coca-Cola.

"Our crops are dead," says Auntie Fine-Fine.

"And our children are hungry," adds Mama B.

"And our men have been poisoned by the factory." Mama sobs.

The President nods and nods. And one of his people writes the whole thing down.

"All of this will be rectified," the President says. "With the funds we have confiscated from Chief Temi-Tola, there is enough to restore and repair all this. There is even enough for international university scholarships for your children.

And of course the factory will be closed."

"No!" Grandfather opens his mouth and speaks at last. "We need the factory. We need jobs for our people. But that factory cannot be allowed to poison everything. You must pay the people who are supposed to inspect it!"

The President bows his head. "This time," he says, "the right thing will be done."

"And I will give No. 1 a phone," says Mr Johnson loudly. "So that he can record the right thing being done. There are thirty million people who want to know what is happenning here."

I jump up and punch the air. A phone!
A phone for me!

The President sighs. Then he shakes
hands with Grandfather. He gets into his
car and the convoy drives away. I count
more than ten cars.

Then somebody
throws me into
the air again. It is
Uncle Go-Easy.
He is calling me
a hero. The
whole village
is calling me
a hero. Even
Grandmother.
But what did
I do? It was thirty million
people who solved this problem. Thirty
million people who cared about this poor
village lost in the bush.

And now, because of them, I will not only go to school, I will also go to super school – to university!

And there I will undoubtedly see so many No. 1 cars that I will be running up and down the roads like a chicken, trying to see them all.

And there I will undoubtedly meet so many people – young people like me, and old people like Prof. And to all those people I will introduce myself as No. 1, the No. 1 car spotter from my village.

But I will tell them that I have not forgotten – and I will never forget – that we are all No. 1. Because together we are the No. 1 solution to all the problems of this whole wide world.

HOORAY!

Atinuke was born in Nigeria
and grew up in both Africa and the UK.
She works as a traditional oral storyteller
in schools and theatres all over the world.
All of Atinuke's many children's books
are set in the Africa of her childhood.
Atinuke lives on a mountain
overlooking the sea in West Wales
with her two fabulous sons.

Warwick Johnson Cadwell
lives by the Sussex seaside with his
smashing family and pets. Most of
his time is spent drawing, or thinking
about drawing, but for a change of
scenery he also skippers boats.
The No. 1 Car Spotter Fights the Factory
is his eighth book for Walker Books.